KT-408-389

25/5

This Topsy and Tim book belongs to

_____

C015074207

Topsy and Tim
Safety First

By Jean and Gareth Adamson

Illustrations by Belinda Worsley

A catalogue record for this book is available from the British Library

Published by Ladybird Books Ltd
A Penguin Company
Penguin Books Ltd., 80 Strand, London WC2R 0RL, UK
Penguin Books Australia Ltd., Camberwell, Victoria, Australia
Penguin Group (NZ) 67 Apollo Drive, Rosedale, North Shore 0632, New Zealand (a division of Pearson NZ Ltd)

001 –
1 3 5 7 9 10 8 6 4 2

© Jean and Gareth Adamson MMXI

The moral rights of the author/illustrator have been asserted
LADYBIRD and the device of a ladybird are trademarks of Ladybird Books Ltd
All rights reserved. No part of this publication may be reproduced, stored in a retrieval system, or transmitted
in any form or by any means, electronic, mechanical, photocopying, recording or otherwise, without the
prior consent of the copyright owner.

ISBN: 978-1-40930-882-9
Printed in China

www.topsyandtim.com

Topsy and Tim were excited. They were going to tea with their friend, Josie Miller, and they were wearing their nice, new trainers.

Topsy and Tim skipped along ahead of Mummy.
One of Topsy's laces came undone and Tim trod on it.
"Don't do that!" shouted Topsy.

Mummy caught up with them and tied
Topsy's laces properly.
"Now hold tight to my hands, keep away
from the kerb and stay safe," she said.

"This is a very busy road," said Mummy.
"We must find a safe crossing."
"Look, there are traffic lights," said Tim.
When they reached the traffic lights a red man was
showing. That meant WAIT – DON'T CROSS.

Topsy pressed the button and soon the traffic stopped. The green man showed them they should cross now. He beeped to hurry them up.

Josie was pleased to see Topsy and Tim.
"Let's play football in the garden," she said.
Josie's little brother Jamie wanted to play too. Tim
kicked the ball high in the air and Jamie ran after it.

"Mind the pond, Jamie," shouted Topsy.
Then she saw the strong grille over the water.
"That's to stop Jamie falling in," said Josie.

Jamie kicked the ball. It rolled into a flower bed and
Topsy ran to find it. She reached in among the flowers.
Something buzzed round her face. It was a bee.

"Go away! Go away!" cried Topsy, flapping her hands.
"Stay still," said Josie, "then it won't sting you."
Topsy did what Josie said and the bee buzzed off.
"You're safe now, Topsy," said Josie.

"What's Jamie doing?" said Tim.
Jamie was holding a little red berry.
"Sweetie?" he said.
"No!" shouted Topsy, Tim and Josie
all together.

"You must never eat anything you find in the garden," said Josie. "It might be poisonous."
Jamie opened his mouth to show them that he hadn't eaten any berries.

It was nearly time for tea, so they all went indoors to wash their hands. Tim undid the stair gate and Topsy helped Jamie to climb the stairs.

Josie made sure that the water was not too hot and they all washed their hands.

Tim wanted to look out of the bathroom window.
"Be careful, Tim," said Josie. "It isn't safe to lean
out of windows."
"I know," said Tim. "I wasn't going to."

Tim ran out of the bathroom and held the door shut. "Let us out, Tim," shouted Josie. "It's dangerous to play with doors. Someone's fingers could get trapped."

It was nearly teatime. Josie's mum was cooking a stir-fry. Topsy and Tim went to look.

"Don't stand near the cooker, twins," she said. "It's very hot and you might burn yourselves."

"Oh no!" said Josie. "Mum, I've spilt my milk."

Josie's mum turned off the electric rings and went to fetch a mop from her cleaning cupboard. Inside the cupboard were all the things she needed to keep the house clean.

"What a lot of bottles!" said Topsy.
"All very poisonous!" said Josie's mum.
"That's why I keep the cupboard door locked."

After tea Josie and Tim watched a DVD while Topsy and Jamie played on the floor. Josie's mum switched on the electric fire and made sure the fireguard was safely fixed.

Topsy saw Jamie putting something else
into his mouth. It was a tiny toy.
"Spit it out, Jamie," she said. "You could
swallow it and choke."
Josie's mum was very pleased with Topsy.

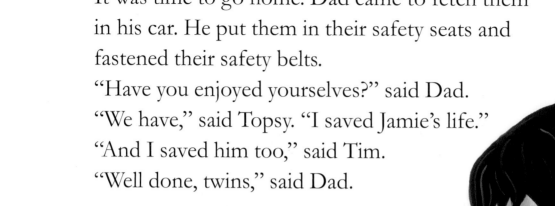

It was time to go home. Dad came to fetch them
in his car. He put them in their safety seats and
fastened their safety belts.

"Have you enjoyed yourselves?" said Dad.

"We have," said Topsy. "I saved Jamie's life."

"And I saved him too," said Tim.

"Well done, twins," said Dad.

*Now turn the page and help
Topsy and Tim solve a puzzle.*

Can you help Topsy and Tim remember which things are safe and which things aren't? Point to the things that could be dangerous.

A Map of the Village

farm

Topsy and
Tim's house

Tony's
house

Kerry's
house

park

garage

post office

health centre

church

primary school

nursery school

police station

Look out for other titles in the series.

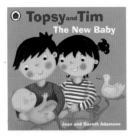 Topsy and Tim — The New Baby

 Topsy and Tim — Have a Birthday Party

 Topsy and Tim — Go on an Aeroplane — Jean and Gareth Adamson

 Topsy and Tim — Play Football — Jean and Gareth Adamson

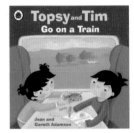 Topsy and Tim — Go on a Train — Jean and Gareth Adamson

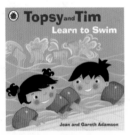 Topsy and Tim — Learn to Swim — Jean and Gareth Adamson

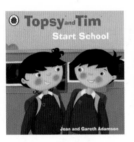 Topsy and Tim — Start School — Jean and Gareth Adamson

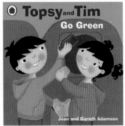 Topsy and Tim — Go Green — Jean and Gareth Adamson

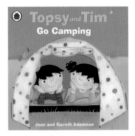 Topsy and Tim — Go Camping — Jean and Gareth Adamson

 Topsy and Tim — Go to Hospital — Jean and Gareth Adamson

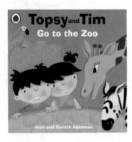 Topsy and Tim — Go to the Zoo — Jean and Gareth Adamson

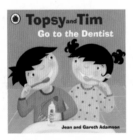 Topsy and Tim — Go to the Dentist — Jean and Gareth Adamson

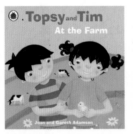 Topsy and Tim — At the Farm — Jean and Gareth Adamson

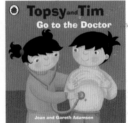 Topsy and Tim — Go to the Doctor — Jean and Gareth Adamson

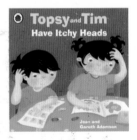 Topsy and Tim — Have Itchy Heads — Jean and Gareth Adamson

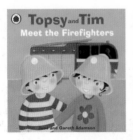 Topsy and Tim — Meet the Firefighters — Jean and Gareth Adamson

 Topsy and Tim — Meet the Police — Jean and Gareth Adamson

 Topsy and Tim — Safety First — Jean and Gareth Adamson

 Available on the App Store

The Ladybird Topsy and Tim app can be downloaded from the App Store.